To Samantha

Have a great time an camp

We love you !

Love

to

DEAN

On the Wings of the Swan

For Samantha, ♡

With the very finest wishes
Love,
Rosemarie Hulla

THE TREASURY OF THE LOST SCROLLS
SERIES INCLUDES

On the Wings of the Swan

The Order of the Azure Star

The River's Reach

On the Wings of the Swan

Written by Rosemarie Gulla

Illustrated by Gary Undercuffler

Alazar Press · Carrboro, NC

Book Design by *Ann Marie Newell, www.newelldesign.com*
Production by *BW&A Books, Inc., www.bwabooks.com*
Edited by Jacqueline K. Ogburn
Printed in Canada by Friesens Corp.
The text and display type of this book is set in Goudy Old Style

Library of Congress Control Number 2007929791
ISBN 978-0-9793000-0-4

First Edition, 2007
10 9 8 7 6 5 4 3 2 1

an imprint of Royal Swan Enterprises, Inc.
201 Orchard Lane, Carrboro, NC 27510
Visit us at *www.royal-swan-enterprises.com*

To my husband, Joseph,
and our three daughters,
Mary Elizabeth, Kathryn Rose, and Megan Anne,
in honor of all that love makes possible.
—*Rosemarie Gulla*

For Diana, my sweetheart.
—*Gary Undercuffler*

AUTHOR'S NOTE
This story was written with the art of the storyteller in mind.
Attention to the read aloud qualities of this book will help bring this tale to life.

Deep within the primal wood
A traveler came and found
A cave wherein there lay closed tight
A chest upon the ground.

Upon examination
His searching eye could see
No trace of recent effort
To claim this mystery.

Forgotten, ancient treasures
Ran coursing through his mind.
What brought him to this lonely place?
What was he now to find?

He poked and pushed and prodded.
No lock did guard the way.
The years alone had sealed tight
The contents 'til this day.

With careful hands, he reached inside
And brought into the light
The treasures from this ancient chest
Long hidden from all sight.

Assembled were forgotten scrolls
Magnificent in form.
He carefully unwrapped the first
And with its words was borne . . .

SCROLL ONE
The River's Gold

Once upon a time the mighty River of Gold flowed freely through the land. It rolled by countless towns and villages, by hills and mountains, by farms and forests. Its water was cool, clean and clear.

Magical creatures, such as the Queen of Wishes, once lived along this river. The Queen of Wishes was named Orella and she loved to be near the people she served. There came a time, however, when Orella had to leave her beloved river. Before leaving, she wished a great treasure of gold into the water, promising that it would be found by "the one who needs it most of all."

Years went by without any sign of Orella. No one saw any gold in the water. People came to believe that Orella had never really existed. It was the children, who could well imagine such a treasure and such a promise, who kept the stories of Orella alive. Some of the villagers humored the children with knowing smiles and feigned interest. Others told them not to speak of such things.

A grumbly, grumpy, grouchy old man also called this place home. He was a man who stepped on flowers and snarled at children. He was a man who sneered at the sun. He lived on the dark side of the mountain.

Sweeping by the bottom of this mountain was the River of Gold as it threaded its way through the nearby village. Every day, the grumbly, grumpy, grouchy old man made his way down the mountain, across the road, along the path, to the River of Gold. He didn't come to drink its sparkling water. He didn't come to bathe. He came to look for Orella's promise — the great treasure of gold.

A young girl named Merryrose lived just beyond the village near the River of Gold. Her father was a weaver and her mother was a seamstress. Merryrose was a bit of both. Early one morning, she wove her long golden hair into a beautiful braid, gathered her needle, fabric and scissors, and set off to practice her stitches. Happily, she skipped toward her favorite spot on the other side of the river.

She danced her way across the bridge, enjoying the echoes of her steps on the wooden planks. But, midway across, she heard a cry for help. It was the grumbly, grumpy, grouchy old man — caught in the swirling water.

Merryrose did not know what to do. The currents swirled swiftly in this part of the river. She pleaded aloud, "Oh, please don't let him drown. What can I do? I wish I could save him."

Reaching to cling to something, the grumbly, grumpy, grouchy old man yelled, "Help me! Somebody help me!" He slapped at the water in panic. Suddenly, Merryrose knew just what to do. She grabbed her scissors, and without a second thought, she snipped off her long golden braid.

She braced herself against the bridge and dangled the braid above him. Frantically, he grabbed and missed. She stretched farther and he caught hold. The river tossed him about but Merryrose carefully moved across the bridge, pulling him toward the bank. She held on tightly, letting go and collapsing with relief when he finally reached the shore. She was trembling. Her heart was pounding. Her mind was racing. She had saved the old man. Then, she watched while he simply, silently walked away. Without a thank you, without a look, he trudged back to his home on the dark side of the mountain. Too shaken to move, Merryrose watched him leave with her braid in his hands.

Merryrose touched what remained of her hair. What had she done? She sat there on the little bridge, confused and upset. She unlaced her shoes as she worked to untangle her thoughts. She walked down to the water's sunny shore. The water licked her toes while the sun warmed her body.

She stared at the river, the River of Gold. "What had he been doing here? Wasn't he lucky I was here? Didn't he realize I cut off my own hair to save him? Why didn't he thank me? Why didn't he look at me? Why did he take my hair?" Her thoughts dissolved into tears. Through the diluted vision of tearful eyes, she saw movement on the water. She blinked into focus a Swan — a magnificent Swan.

A crown of jewels sat upon the Swan's head. The gems reflected the sun's light and their brilliance heralded the arrival of this majestic creature. Merryrose stared. Then she stepped closer, into the water. The Swan came directly to her and bent low at her feet. Without hesitation, Merryrose reached out to touch its feathers. The Swan suddenly arched its body and flapped its great wings sweeping Merryrose onto its back. She grabbed on and held tightly as the Swan lifted and took to the air. She squeezed her eyes shut. When she dared to look, the world below seemed remarkably small. It all looked so different from the wings of the Swan.

SCROLL TWO
Casimiria is Revealed

The Swan soared while Merryrose held fast. She saw a land beyond the clouds. The Swan flew farther and farther into this beautiful land, so obviously its home. Now, she could not even think about closing her eyes.

Everything brightened wherever the Swan flew but a dark shadowy mist followed their radiant path. "What is that?" she asked aloud. The mist responded.

"It is Drufia. My name is Drufia. You have meddled into things beyond your understanding and my warning to you couldn't be more serious. Do nothing while you are here and take nothing from this place when you leave." Merryrose shuddered at the steely coolness of the voice, the voice of Drufia.

Merryrose, still holding tightly to the Swan's neck, saw a sparkling, a twinkling, just under the gloom. She heard singing too, coming from below the misty darkness, and this eased her mind.

"Snuff, smother, suffocate
Destroying all you could.
Leave us now. We don't care how.
Our wish is that you would.

Insisting on your presence
Threatens all that's good.
Leave now! Never come this way.
Leave now! Understood?"

The mist cleared. Then, the Swan twisted and dropped Merryrose directly into the lap of a short, but not so diminutive, winged creature. "Oh, good, help at last," said the little winged one as she fell backward, pretending to faint. "Here, hold the wand and please get off my tummy so I can roll myself right." The Swan rose back into the sky.

Merryrose tumbled onto the grass with the wand. It glittered and sparkled in her hand. "I — ," began Merryrose, "can't believe I'm — you're — here," finished the fairy and Merryrose in unison. The magical being laughed and introduced herself as Munya. "First, let me help you up. Then, please give me back my wand."

Munya was as wide as she was tall. Like a ball, she spun her round body about, whisking sparkles out of the air and securing them in a little silver box in her right hand. As she worked, she chanted with delight:

"Welcome to the Land of Wishes!
Such a well-wisher you are.
Working wealth out of the water
When you saved old Alazar.

A man in search of treasure
Does not ever look in vain.
You wished the wish to save him
Giving back to him his name."

Merryrose understood little of that but she understood enough to ask, "There really is a Land of Wishes?"

"There really is a Land of Wishes," declared Munya.

"I am — am i-in the Land of Wishes?" stammered Merryrose. Munya fluttered up to come nose-to-nose with Merryrose and stated matter-of-factly, "You are in the Land of Wishes. A wish once wished comes here. This is Casimiria."

"C-Casimiria," repeated Merryrose with a hesitating nod. Munya flitted about brandishing her little wand against the darkness singing:

"What so often is forgotten,
Or not really understood,
Are the causes of the problems
And the reasons for the good.

It is here dear, oh yes, here dear
That whatever one has wished
Gathers with one's other wishes
In a kind of . . . mixing dish.

No matter how we mix them,
All the recipes depend
On the quality of wishes
That the wisher wished to send.

We're like a great big mirror.
What we see is what you get.
You serve it up. We dish it back.
Fare's fair and no regret."

"So many of the wishes we receive have not the shimmer and shine of yours, dear." Munya displayed the silver wish box. "I heard your wish to save the grumbly, grumpy, grouchy old man. It came directly to me:

"The very finest wishes

Into my wish box go."

Dreamily, with eyes closed and a half-smile on her fairy face, Munya sighed:

"A sacrifice — at such high price.

A masterpiece, you know."

"Please, tell me more," asked Merryrose. "I don't really understand why I am in the Land of Wishes."

With great respect, Munya continued, "Orella has been waiting for one like you, someone with a heart of gold, to release the treasure from the river." Munya whispered, "Orella wants you to have the Golden Key." With that, two wee fairies popped into view and Munya handed them her silver wish box and wand. Munya produced a rather unusual Golden Key. She held the Golden Key in front of Merryrose's face as if measuring something. Merryrose watched Munya and the Golden Key intently.

With a clap of thunder, a rumble and a roar, Drufia declared from the mist, "The silver wish box in my hands will end things right here."

The two wee fairies gasped but Munya worked quickly. With her hands on both ends of the Golden Key, Munya squeezed it to a smaller size and handed the beautiful Golden Key to Merryrose. A burst of darkness obscured the wish box, the wand and the two wee fairies. Merryrose called out, "No! I wish the Land of Wishes to be safe and protected right now."

The darkness dissolved revealing the silver box, the wand and the two relieved wee fairies. "You are in Orella's Land of Wishes, Drufia, and you have no power against the Golden Key," warned Munya. "Leave us."

Munya threaded a ribbon through the end of the Golden Key and tied it about Merryrose's neck as she said:

> *"This precious, precious Golden Key*
> *Unlocks a heart closed tight.*
> *Please take it now. You will know how!*
> *So, go and set things right."*

With great flourish, Munya ascended to announce to all of Casimiria:

> *"The treasure of the river is released!*
> *A heart of gold lives on and will not cease."*

And then, whispering to Merryrose:

> *"There will be those to stop you.*
> *Great powers will you see.*
> *Let nothing seen alarm you.*
> *You have the Golden Key."*

Merryrose touched the Golden Key around her neck. Moving it from one hand to the other, she fingered its pattern, texture and form. "What does it open?" she asked, quite entranced by this fabulous Golden Key.

"Hearts," replied Munya. "It opens hearts."

Merryrose held the Golden Key tightly and sighed, "Will I really be safe from Drufia?" No one answered. Merryrose looked up and saw hundreds of fairies in attendance. There were fairies from every corner of the world.

Munya smiled, "They have all come to witness the presentation of the Golden Key and they will keep you safe."

The two wee fairies continued to guard the silver wish box and Munya's wand as Munya adjusted the Golden Key for Merryrose and touched her golden hair. At the return of the Swan, the fairies bowed their heads and cleared a path to Merryrose.

The Swan bent low at her feet and Merryrose climbed onto its back. She was whisked away, out of Casimiria, to the cheering of the fairies. Drufia, however, trailed behind them all the way to the River of Gold. Munya watched with concern as she took back her silver wish box and wand. Gently, Munya tapped the two wee fairies on their little heads in thanks.

Merryrose landed with both feet on the ground. With the Golden Key resting safely about her neck, she watched the Swan leave. She gathered up her sewing things scattered about the bridge as she heard Munya's voice singing. She looked about but saw nothing. Clearly, as if she was right there, she heard Munya speak:

"We can all be taught to sew
And mend the finest cloth.
But the fabric that needs mending
Is the fabric of our thought.

The wishes that you think to wish
Are those that can repair —
Providing alterations
Using strands of golden hair."

Just then, as quickly as thoughts come and go, all of her luxurious hair was back. The sun had not moved across the sky since she stood in the river and first saw the Swan. Not a moment had passed. "Did all of this happen in an instant?" she wondered aloud as she stroked her long braid. Merryrose stood still and held the Golden Key saying, "I wish the old man could feel how it feels to be kind." She pulled her braid in front of her face and giggled. Merryrose hurried home, marveling at all that had happened.

15

SCROLL THREE
"For the Welfare of Others…"

Meanwhile, in a little shack on the dark side of the mountain, the grumbly, grumpy, grouchy old man held the golden braid as he grimaced and groaned. "A handful of golden hair! Puhhh!! All I want is the treasure. All I search for is the treasure and what I get is this fool's measure of gold. Aghh!! It will bring some kind of price at the market but the river holds its treasure far too long."

As the old man held the braid in his hands, it grew heavier and heavier. Golden hair, strand by strand, was changing into solid gold. The braid in the grumbly, grumpy,

grouchy old man's hands became much too heavy to hold. He dropped the gold on the table. The man who never smiled, danced around the room.

It wasn't long before the grumbly, grumpy, grouchy old man was seen about town. Unaccustomed to errands, he spoke brusquely to a few shop-keepers but many noticed him as he broke off bits of the golden strands to be weighed for payment. The gold was pure and dazzling. "What is going on?" they all wondered. "Is there gold in the mountains? Did he keep this gold hidden for all these years? Who remembers when he first came to live on the mountain?" These people paid attention to him and the grumbly, grumpy, grouchy old man was uncomfortable under the weight of it.

He decided to have some decent clothes made that might make him less noticeable. He quickly crossed the bridge over the River of Gold, thinking not one thought about what had happened there. He stomped up to the house, the house of the seamstress, the weaver and their daughter, Merryrose.

Merryrose kept out of sight as her mother fit the fabric on the grumbly, grumpy, grouchy old man. With one hand, he fingered the strands of gold in his old pockets. With his other hand, he fingered the new cloth. He would not pay her until the suit was ready. When the seamstress finished with her measuring, the old man unexpectedly caught a glimpse of his reflection in a mirror. He straightened his back to stand tall. Maybe the people would not recognize him in his new clothes. He quickly turned his face away. He muttered and mumbled and walked out the door. He crossed the bridge over the River of Gold once again as he headed home. Merryrose wondered what she should be doing with this Golden Key of hers.

The day came for the old man to return to the seamstress. Without speaking, he dropped some golden strands on a table and grunted his approval when the seamstress brought out his new clothes. They fit him perfectly and he left carrying his old clothes in a bundle under his arm. Merryrose stayed out of sight.

The seamstress held the golden strands in her hands. She rolled the heavy, dazzling gold back and forth as she remarked, "What a strange, sad, old man!" Merryrose felt for the ribbon around her neck and patted the Golden Key. "I wish I knew what to do to set things right," wished Merryrose.

The old man walked home in silence. He was still a man without gratitude. He trudged up the side of the mountain, passing a familiar beggar on the way. When the beggar entreated the grumbly, grumpy, grouchy old man to give him something, the old man growled, "Here!" and tossed the old bundle of clothes in his direction. When the bundle hit him, the beggar was instantly dressed in new, warm clothing.

"Thank you, kind sir," the beggar excitedly called out to the grumbly, grumpy, grouchy old man who never looked up.

"Leave me alone," he snarled. Later, the beggar told everyone of the old man's kindness when in fact, there had been none.

Some people began to follow the grumbly, grumpy, grouchy old man as he went about his daily business. In their eyes, he was instantly and mysteriously rich. Now, he was showing signs of generosity. They were even mentioning the possibility of the treasure of gold in the river. "Imagine that!" speculated some of the townsfolk. The children were intrigued.

The Golden Key was changing everything. Somehow now, everything the old man did on behalf of himself was miraculously extended for the welfare of others. People were noticing him, speaking of him — and speaking to him. He rarely spoke back. He was thinking however, and his thinking led him to some unexpected memories. The small group, who had first paid attention to him, grew into crowds who followed him everywhere. A distant memory surfaced. He remembered great throngs of people around him and he struggled to give them faces and names.

Once accustomed to hunger, the poorest people in this town feasted for the first time in their lives because when the old man ate, everyone ate. Magically, food appeared for all who gathered near him. When he climbed between warm covers at night, everyone grew comfortable. Magically, everyone outside his mountain shack was snug and warm. The people began to tell all who would listen of the old man's powers and kindnesses. The grumbly, grumpy, grouchy old man should not have received such thanks. His heart remained closed.

"I wish the powers of the Golden Key would free the old man's heart," wished Merryrose aloud as she heard the stories of his kindnesses. Munya caught her wish and smiled.

"Meddlesome girl," hissed Drufia as she worked her wickedness from deep within the ground and within the depths of the River of Gold. Her sinister interests in the grumbly, grumpy, grouchy old man began when she had captured him as a young man, a young king. She defeated his armies, collapsed his rule and scattered confusion in its place. "I will not let Orella get in my way now."

Drufia's powers had grown strong enough to cast darkness into Casimiria itself, keeping wishes and dreams unseen and unfulfilled. "I was ready to deal the fatal blow to all of Casimiria. Orella and her Golden Key mustn't stop me. I may not have the Golden Key but I can conceal it. I will transform that Golden Key into. . . . " she paused to consider. She tapped her elegant fingers together, adjusted her hood, and turned on her heels. "Just as I can travel lighter than air, a swan's feather will do rather nicely in this case." A derisive laugh escaped Drufia's lips. The River of Gold swirled like a drain about to swallow anyone daring to seek Orella's true treasure.

The people were praising, blessing and thanking the grumbly, grumpy, grouchy old man. They were changing their own selfish ways because of him — and Drufia could not rest while she worked to foil Orella's plan. She could not, would not rest, now that the grumbly, grumpy, grouchy old man was finding his way out of the darkness. Drufia made her own kind of wish to keep the old man angry and mean and resolved to stay that way. "Keep the gold for yourself. Keep it all."

Despite the force of Drufia's powers, the river's treasure was unlike anything the old man had ever known. He allowed himself to think about that day in the river. He decided to go back to the bridge. Drufia, determined to keep what she had taken, raced to the depths of the river.

The grumbly, grumpy, grouchy old man walked into the water of the River of Gold. "Fool's gold — braid of hair — fool of a girl cut it off. Stupid! It turned to gold — my gold. In my hands, it turned to gold. In my hands, a treasure." Then, he let the thought in. "It was her golden braid." Drufia's wail touched off a small rumbling of the earth.

Gratitude in a selfish heart is a strange thing. The feeling confused and delighted the old man. He wanted to find the girl. The people told him about Merryrose — who still had her long, golden braid.

The old man made his way to the home of the seamstress, the weaver and Merryrose. As Merryrose opened the door, the startled old man stepped back. He saw her long, golden, flowing hair. Merryrose put her hand on his and called him by his name. "Alazar, I know your name."

He grew faint at the sound. He sat down outside her door. Merryrose grabbed both of his hands in hers as she knelt down in front of him. "Your name has been given back to you. The treasure you wished for is yours. See, I have the Golden Key. It opens hearts closed tight — like yours, Alazar — like yours."

Alazar slowly shook his head and sat upright. His eyes narrowed and focused on Merryrose and the Golden Key. "This is none of my own doing. You did this," he said.

"Hmm, somehow, I did," admitted Merryrose with a wide, brilliant smile. Holding the Golden Key tightly in her hand, Merryrose told Alazar, "Make the wish, right now, that is dearest to your heart."

Alazar's face started to smile. "If this is what kindness can do then I wish that kindness was truly a part of me." He laughed. His whole face softened. The sound of his own laugh, once hidden as deeply as the river's treasure, made him laugh even more.

Alazar laughed and spoke with Merryrose for some time. "I've been to the Land of Wishes," began Merryrose.

"So, there really is a Land of Wishes," said the smiling Alazar.

"Oh, yes. There really is a Land of Wishes with fairies, wands, a silver wish box and a Golden Key," said Merryrose. They chuckled together as Merryrose spoke of Munya and they marveled together as she spoke of the presentation of the Golden Key. She told of the royal Swan, the misty darkness and the voice of Drufia.

"Did you say Drufia was in Casimiria?" asked a visibly alarmed Alazar. "Drufia is able to . . . " Alazar paused, "have powers here and in Casimiria too?"

"Alazar, I have heard the stories of Drufia who forced Orella out of this land as she destroyed the kingdom of the great King Alazar. Drufia's the one who. . . . " Her voice trailed off as she realized who this old Alazar — sitting in front of her — really was.

"Merryrose, I am King Alazar," he announced flatly. Alazar's memory had returned.

"You are King Alazar! You have been here all the time but your heart has been closed! We thought you had been killed. Everyone knows of the great battles you fought." King Alazar listened to Merryrose but remained thoughtful, being well acquainted with the malevolence of Drufia.

"They are opposites, they are. Drufia and Orella are opposites," instructed King Alazar. "Keep that in mind. Orella left this place but kept a powerful wish hidden within the promise of a treasure of gold. You see, your generous wish to help me at a cost to yourself, invoked Orella's wish allowing the true treasure . . . "

" . . . to be found by the one who needs it most of all," finished Merryrose.

King Alazar continued, "I have been under Drufia's power for all of this time and now, I am released because of you and Orella. Drufia will be on the move now. What did she say to you in Casimiria?"

Merryrose recalled the words of Drufia, "You have meddled into things beyond your understanding and my warning to you couldn't be more serious. Do nothing while you are here and take nothing from this place when you leave."

"Did you see her?" asked King Alazar.

"No, I only heard her voice. She was the misty darkness in that bright and beautiful place," replied Merryrose.

"Drufia destroys and she will destroy again," said King Alazar. "Someday, you will face her. You must always remember what Orella has been able to do with your help. You, Merryrose, have the Golden Key and I, King Alazar, have returned."

Merryrose watched King Alazar leave her house. He talked to the flowers. He laughed with the children. He saluted the sun.

Merryrose smiled as she closed the door. "I wish . . . " she began, when a blast of air threw the door wide open. Alarmed, Merryrose grabbed the Golden Key, which transformed into a large feather, a swan's feather, right in her hands. A second blast of air stole the feather out of her hands and sent it sailing on the wind. Merryrose chased the feather outside and saw the royal Swan waiting. A strong wind shook the very walls of her house and a thick black mist rose up from the ground and came through the cracks. Merryrose flew away on the wings of the Swan. She flew in pursuit of the feather.